To Amanda Cockrell—thanks for making
the Hollins children's literature graduate program
way bigger and much better. We will miss you!
—C.R.

For Matthew, Michael, and Emily
(and M & G always).
Your birthdays are my favorite days.
—C.G.

Text copyright © 2018 by Candice Ransom
Jacket art and interior illustrations copyright © 2018 by Christine Grove

Visit us on the Web! rhcbooks.com

Educators and librarians, for a variety of teaching tools, visit us at RHTeachersLibrarians.com

Library of Congress Cataloging-in-Publication Data is available upon request.
ISBN 978-1-5247-6819-5 (trade) — ISBN 978-1-5247-6820-1 (lib. bdg.) — ISBN 978-1-5247-6821-8 (ebook)

MANUFACTURED IN CHINA
10 9 8 7 6 5 4 3 2 1
First Edition

Amanda Panda

AND THE BIGGER, BETTER BIRTHDAY

by Candice Ransom
illustrated by Christine Grove

DOUBLEDAY BOOKS FOR YOUNG READERS

Tomorrow is Amanda Panda's birthday. She will be the first one in Ms. Lemon's kindergarten to have a birthday. That makes her special. And she will be the first one in her class to be six years old. That makes her famous. She can't wait to invite her friends to her party on Saturday. The theme is School Bus.

Amanda hurries to the bus stop. She
wants to give Bitsy the first invitation.

Bitsy is her best friend.
Their teacher says they
never stop talking.
They sit side by side on
the story rug and talk.

They talk during naptime.

They talk on the swings at recess.

Bitsy rushes over to Amanda. She is wearing a poufy
skirt that makes rustling sounds.

"How come you're dressed up?" Amanda asks.

"Because today is my birthday," says Bitsy. "I'm six!"

Amanda's tummy feels lower than her knees. Bitsy's birthday is today? *Bitsy* is six?

"And I brought sparkle princess cupcakes for the whole class!" Bitsy says.

This cannot be happening.

At school, Ms. Lemon has decorated the classroom. "It's Bitsy's special day," she says "Let's all sing 'Happy Birthday.'"

Everyone sings except Amanda.

Ms. Lemon points to the calendar. "Tomorrow is Amanda's birthday. We'll sing that song again tomorrow morning."

Amanda does not want a leftover song on *her* special day.

HAPPY BIRTHDAY, BITSY!

Amanda wanders over to the calendar wall.

Somehow the dates get changed.

"Look!" Amanda says. "It's really *my* birthday today!"

Ms. Lemon frowns. "Amanda, you know that's not true.
Fix the calendar, please."

Bitsy hands out her cupcakes.

"There are enough for your birthday, too," she says to Amanda.

Amanda does not want leftover cupcakes on *her* special day.

Amanda wanders over to the nature corner.

Somehow the class hamster winds up with a cupcake.

"Whiskers wants to celebrate, too," Amanda says.

Ms. Lemon removes the cupcake from the cage.

"Hamsters don't do birthdays," says Ms. Lemon.

Next, Bitsy passes out glittery cards.

"Everybody is invited to my party on Saturday,"
she says. "The theme is Princess Kitten."

"*My* party is on Saturday!" Amanda yells. "And the theme is
School Bus!"

"I can't go to two parties," James says.

"A School Bus party doesn't sound like much fun," adds Molly.

Amanda's tummy feels lower than her toes.

"And we're going to have an ice cream sundae buffet!" Bitsy says.

This cannot be happening.

"Change the day of your party," Amanda tells Bitsy.
"I'm the oldest," says Bitsy. "Have *your* party on Sunday!"
Amanda does not want a leftover party day.

Amanda wanders over to the pencil sharpener.

Somehow her invitation from Bitsy ends up in the trash.

"You're not coming to my party?" Bitsy asks.

"I don't do birthdays," says Amanda.

Amanda and Bitsy stop talking to each other.
They are no longer best friends.
They sit far apart on the story rug.

They do not whisper during naptime.

They ignore the swings at recess.

On the playground, Amanda plays bus driver by herself. She misses having somebody to talk to. She misses having Bitsy take the passengers' tickets.

Then she hears a rustling sound.

"Stay off my bus," Amanda tells Bitsy. "We're not talking."
"*Not talking* is for little kids," Bitsy says, climbing aboard.
"When you're older like me, you'll understand."

"I'll be older *tomorrow*," says Amanda.

Bitsy sits in the seat behind Amanda. "I can't miss my best friend's birthday," she says. "I'll cancel my party and go to yours on Saturday."

"No, you can't! I'm going to *your* party on Saturday!" protests Amanda.

"No! I'm going to *your* party!" yells Bitsy.

This cannot be happening.

But suddenly, Amanda has an idea. Her tummy feels lighter than a balloon.

HAPPY BIRTHDAY, AMANDA AND BITSY

The double Princess Kitten School Bus
birthday party is a big hit with Amanda's and
Bitsy's friends on Saturday. Princess kittens
ride buses and wave magic wands. Bus drivers
wear sparkly crowns and take passengers to the
Birthday Castle. There are two cakes and two
kinds of ice cream at the sundae buffet . . .

. . . and two best friends, who stop
talking long enough to make a wish.

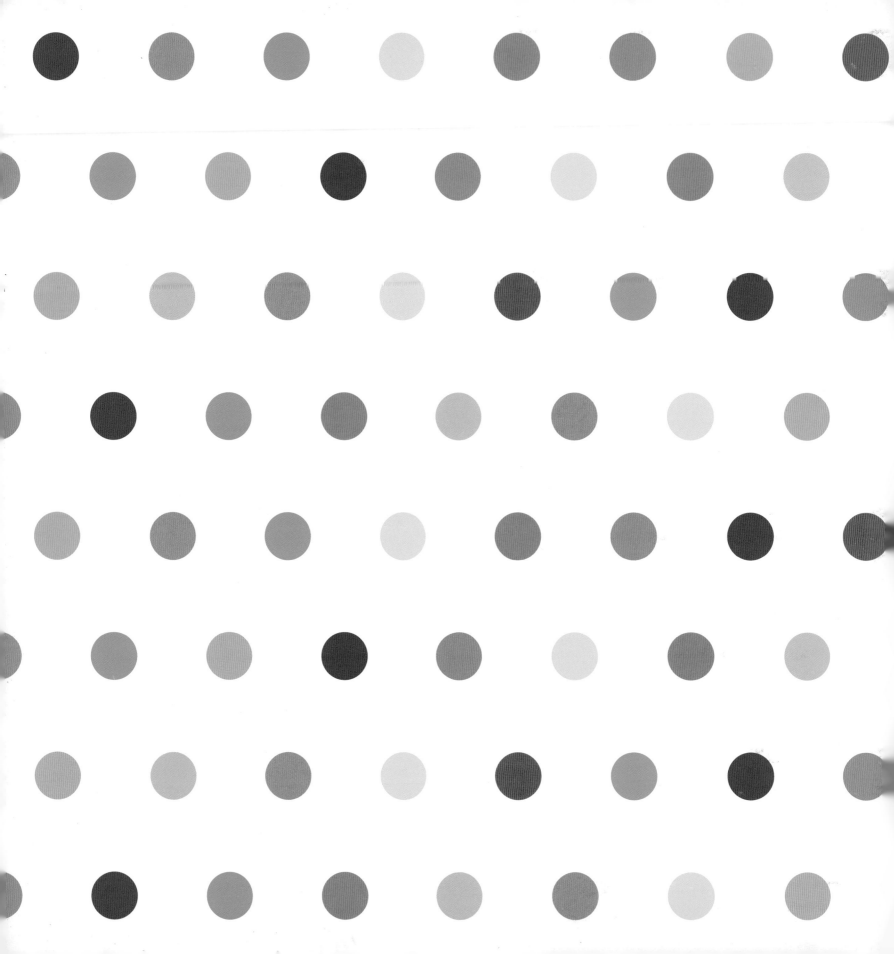